ROAMING with RUDY

Washington DC!

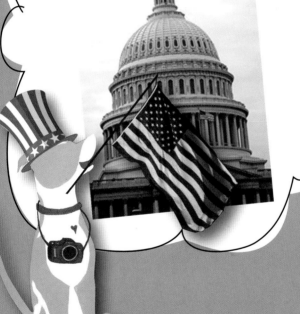

Sage
PRESS

Hey Rudy!
When we go to
Washington, DC,
one of the first things
we'll see is the
United States Capitol!

It's a symbol of democracy and represents a
government based on the wishes of
citizens, and not kings or dictators.
Our first president, George Washington,
laid the cornerstone in 1793.

The Capitol is where the **U.S. CONGRESS** meets. Congress is made up of the Senate and the House of Representatives. Each state elects Congressmen. Congress passes laws and makes decisions about spending and printing money. They can also sign treaties and declare war with other countries.

DID YOU KNOW?

When Congress is in session, flags fly over the chambers. At night, a light burns in the dome.

Inside the ROTUNDA, or dome, the ceiling is decorated with a large mural. It shows President, George Washington, surrounded by the figures of Liberty, Authority and Victory. The 13 maidens in the center represent the original thirteen colonies.

We'll also see large paintings on the walls that illustrate important events in history.

In 1814, the British army set fire to the Capitol and the White House. Luckily, a rainstorm kept it from burning down completely.

The President lives on the upper floors of the **WHITE HOUSE.** Meetings, formal events, and visits with foreign leaders take place on the first floor.

The Oval Office is where the President works.

White House pets have included cats, dogs, racoons, snakes, ponies and goats. Dogs are definitely the most popular, but that's hardly a big surprise, huh, Rudy?

DID YOU KNOW?
George Washington chose the site for the White House, but he's the only president who never got to live there because he left office before it was finished.

The Presidential Seal is the symbol of the presidency. It appears on all official documents and vehicles.

The 13 clouds above the eagle and the red and white stripes on the shield represent the original 13 states. The border has 50 stars, one for each state in the union today. Olive branches in the eagle's claws symbolize peace, and the arrows remind us of the powers of war.

The **Supreme Court** is the highest court in the U.S.

There are nine judges--one Chief Justice and eight Associate Judges. That way, there's never a tie vote.

Supreme Court Judges are nominated by the President and approved by the Senate.

There's lots of tradition in the Supreme Court. All Justices shake hands as they enter the courtoom. This is a reminder that they need to work together, even if they disagree.

EQUAL JUSTICE UNDER LAW

The Library of Congress is the world's LARGEST library! It has over 50 million books, photographs, sheet music and motion pictures. It even has YOUR first book Rudy!

The Gutenberg Bible is one of the most valuable books, and it's displayed here too. It was the first book to be printed with moveable type in 1454.

DID YOU KNOW?

The Library of Congress was the first building in Washington, DC to have electricity.

The Library of Congress is one of the most beautiful buildings in America. At the top of the stairs is a mosaic of Minerva, the Roman Goddess of Knowledge. She holds a scroll that lists all the subjects that are important to civilization.

If we go up a few more steps, we can look down into the Main Reading Room where anyone can go to do research.

DOG DNA by DR. BARKLY

AKC DOG BREEDS

WHAT KIND of DOG ARE YOU?

BIG BLUE BOOK of DOGS

Washington, DC is not a state. It's a FEDERAL DISTRICT.

George Washington chose this spot for the Capitol since it was only 20 miles from his Mt. Vernon home. Virginia and Maryland donated the land.

© openstreetmaps.com

Starting at the Capitol, the city is split into four sections: Northeast, Northwest, Southeast and Southwest. All the streets running north/south are numbered, and the streets going east/west are alphabetical. Some diagonal streets are named after states.

DID YOU KNOW?

Washington, DC's original shape was a square with 10 miles on each side. A boundary stone was placed at every mile point, and some stones are still visible today.

Washington, DC is big, so if we get tired of walking Rudy, there are plenty of other ways to get around!

The METRO is an easy transportation option. To find a station, look for tall black signs with a big "M."

The Metro Rail Trip Planner shows the best metro routes. It also has ticket information and directions to monuments and museums.

Above ground, the Old Town Trolley and Big Bus tours allow us to hop on and off at all the major sites.

The RED CIRCULATOR BUS has routes throughout the city and is used by locals and tourists.

Walking tours, ranger-led bike tours, Segways, and bike rentals from "Capitol Bikeshares" make it easy to cover lots of ground.

The National Mall

The National Mall is a 3-mile long grassy area that goes from the Potomac (Puh-tow-mack) River to Capitol Hill. Many big events have happened here, like war protests and Civil Rights leader Martin Luther King Jr.'s famous "I Have a Dream speech."

DID YOU KNOW?

The National Mall is sometimes called "America's Front Yard."

We can play frisbee, watch the July 4th fireworks or join in the annual Kite Flying Festival.

The Mall is where most of the monuments and memorials are located. And, it's where we'll find the **Smithsonian Museums!**

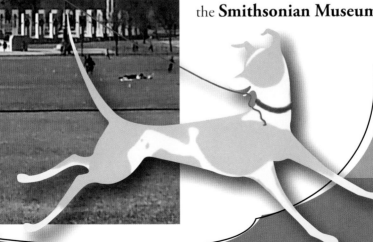

The **SMITHSONIAN MUSEUM** is
the largest museum in the world!

It's actually made up of 19 museums,
9 research centers AND
the National Zoo!

Entrance to all of the
Smithsonian museums
is FREE
thanks to founder,
James Smithson.

Let's start our tour at the
red brick "**Castle**."

This was the original Smithsonian
building. Now it's a visitor center
where we can get information and
a 3-D Planner Map!

DID YOU KNOW?

British scientist James Smithson
never visited the United States.
When he died, he mysteriously left
his huge fortune to create an
institution for sharing knowledge
with American citizens.

One of the most popular and largest of the museums at the Smithsonian is the National Air & Space Museum. We'll learn about the history of flight--from Orville and Wilbur Wright's first airplane to Lindbergh's "Spirit of St. Louis!"

We'll also see war planes from World Wars I and II, like the Sopwith Camel, P-51 Mustangs and Spitfires. There are modern fighter jets too. They even have the plane that test pilot Chuck Yeager flew when he broke the sound barrier!

DID YOU KNOW?

The Smithsonian has the largest collection of historic aircraft and spacecraft in the WORLD! It has over 60,000 objects.

Some of the coolest things to do are the **RIDE SIMULATORS!** Let's climb aboard the Space Shuttle and see what it feels like to live without gravity in the International Space Station.

We can do barrel rolls in an F-18 Super Hornet, experience aerial combat in a World War I bi-plane or an F-86 Super Sabre!

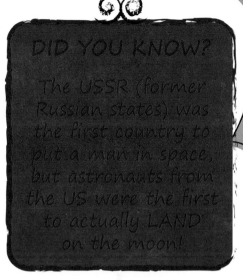

DID YOU KNOW?

The USSR (former Russian states) was the first country to put a man in space, but astronauts from the US were the first to actually LAND on the moon!

There are exhibits about NASA's first Apollo space program. We can try on astronaut suits, climb inside a space capsule, and even touch a REAL MOON ROCK!

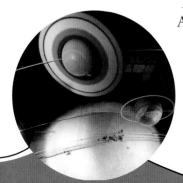

Then we can go to the Einstein Planetarium to learn about planets & galaxies.

Mummies and squids and bears oh my...
Termites, tarantulas and dinosaurs that fly!

At the **Natural History Museum**, check out bugs, butterflies and dinosaur bones.

DID YOU KNOW?
Mammals can control their
body temperature and feed
their babies milk.
Most of them have hair
and do not lay eggs.

We can watch tarantula feedings and crawl through a termite mound. Or, walk into a mine and see the Hope Diamond, the biggest Blue Diamond in the WORLD!

We'll learn all about PACHYDERMS (*pack-uh-derms*) or elephants, in the Elephant Rotunda. At the Koch Hall of Human Origins, exhibits show the skulls of **Neanderthals**, or Cave Men.

In the Ocean Hall, look for the giant squid and the North Atlantic Right Whale named Phoenix. We can even explore a live coral reef!

And, we'll see YOUR favorite exhibit Rudy-- the **Mummified Cats** from Egypt!

DID YOU KNOW?

Tiny algae inside coral gives it its color. When stressed, corals lose the algae and look bleached white

At the **American History Museum**
we'll see the "Star Spangled Banner,"
the American flag that inspired
our national anthem.

We'll learn what
it was like to live
before trains, airplanes
and automobiles...
even before TV!

There are exhibits of
American inventions
like Thomas Edison's
light bulb and
the telegraph.

Items from popular
culture, like the
Muppets, Chef Julia
Child's kitchen and
Muhammed Ali's
boxing gloves are here.
Even Dorothy's ruby
slippers from the
Wizard of OZ
are on display.

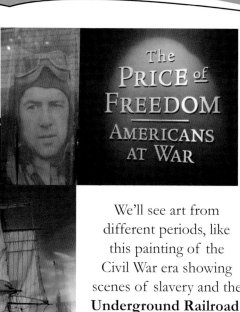

In the "American Ideals" Wing, we'll learn about FREEDOM, and the people that have fought so hard to preserve that freedom.

We'll see art from different periods, like this painting of the Civil War era showing scenes of slavery and the **Underground Railroad.**

One exhibit shows the original lunch counter from a Woolworth's drugstore in Greensboro, NC, the site of a famous Civil Rights sit-in.

DID YOU KNOW?

In 1960, African American students were refused service at a Woolworth's lunch counter. Their quiet protest challenged racial inequality.

"**Philately**" *(phuh-late-lee)* is the study and collection of stamps.

The **National Postal Museum** charts the history of the U.S. Postal system from the "Pony Express to "rail mail." We'll see exhibits ranging from the tiniest stamp to a huge post office bus, and learn how mail is sorted and delivered.

DID YOU KNOW?

The "Inverted Jenny" stamp was printed accidentally with the airplane upside down. Only 100 of these were printed so they are very valuable.

Let's check out the exhibit about "Owney!" Owney was a stray dog who hitched rides on mail trains. Postal workers fed and cared for him, and he became the unofficial mascot of the Railway Mail Service

We all know money doesn't grow on trees, but have you ever wondered where it DOES come from?

At the **Bureau of Engraving & Printing,** we can take a tour and watch money being printed. Money is made using an intaglio (in-tahl-lio) process--an Italian word meaning to cut or engrave.

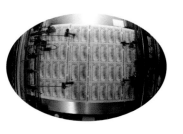

Making money is a big process:

1. First, engravers carve letters or designs into a hard surface.
2. Next, engraved pictures, like the one of Ben Franklin on the $100 bill, are transferred to metal plates.
3. After the plates are made, machines print **20,000** sheets at a time using 14 colors at once.
4. The bills are then inspected, cut and then stacked in piles of 100.
5. Finally, they are packaged and sent to banks and into circulation.

Money is changed every 7-10 years to keep people from making "counterfeit" or fake money. It's printed on special paper and has security features like serial numbers and color-shifting ink.

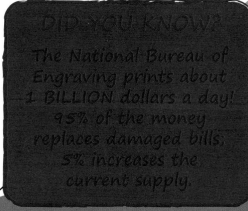

DID YOU KNOW?

The National Bureau of Engraving prints about 1 BILLION dollars a day! 95% of the money replaces damaged bills; 5% increases the current supply.

There are lots of other cool museums in Washington, DC...

The National Gallery of Art & Sculpture Garden

Wealthy art collector Andrew Mellon wanted America to have a major art gallery. He donated his own money and his personal art collection to build the National Gallery of Art. Famous paintings and art from around the world are here. The outdoor garden has fun sculptures like a giant bronze spider and this old-fashioned typewriter eraser.

The National Archives

We'll see the original **Declaration of Independence,** the **US Constitution** and the **Bill of Rights** at this museum. Explore how generations of Americans debated issues like citizenship, free speech, voting rights and equal opportunity.

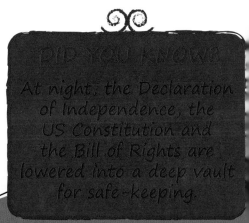

DID YOU KNOW?

At night, the Declaration of Independence, the US Constitution and the Bill of Rights are lowered into a deep vault for safe-keeping.

The National Museum of the American Indian

Discover how early tribes in the Western Hemisphere lived, worked and played. Learn about tipis, igloos, long houses and wigwams. Look for a Lakota buffalo headdress, a birch bark canoe, moccasins, masks and baskets.

Have you heard the phrase,
"Crime Doesn't Pay?"

At the **Museum of Crime & Punishment**, we'll learn about the history of crime and become crime scene investigators or CSI!

There are five galleries where we can help gather evidence for a crime lab, take a lie detector test or join in a high-speed chase.

Try to hack a computer, or escape from a jail cell like this one.

Exhibits highlight "America's Most Wanted" and famous criminals like Bonnie & Clyde--we'll even see their getaway car!

We'll learn about fingerprinting, DNA testing and other forensic science that solves crimes.

If you were a reporter, you'd be telling people about crimes, rather than solving them.

EXTRA! EXTRA!
Read All About It!

Imagine what it was like to learn about events before TV and the internet! "Town Criers" shouted the news to passersby in the 16th century, and later, people heard about what was happening from newspapers and radio.

At the **NEWSEUM,** we'll see headlines from all over the world! One exhibit shows the twisted wreckage of the World Trade Center from September 11.

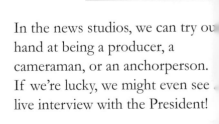

Compare Freedom of Speech in the U.S., or our right to say what we think, to other countries where it's controlled by the government. Learn about journalists that have won the Pulitzer Prize--the highest award in journalism.

In the news studios, we can try ou hand at being a producer, a cameraman, or an anchorperson. If we're lucky, we might even see live interview with the President!

There are film clips of historic events like the fall of the
Berlin Wall, shots of astronauts walking on
the MOON, or scenes of giant
earthquakes and other
natural disasters.

DID YOU KNOW?

The Newseum holds
the largest section
of the Berlin Wall
outside of Germany.

Become a
SPY in TRAINING
at the International
SPY MUSEUM!

We can adopt a secret identity or "cover" and pretend to be someone else. After memorizing details about our fake identity, we'll attempt to pass through security checkpoints like a real spy.

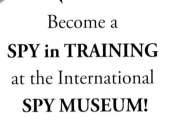

Videos show us the art of disguise--how spies wore wigs and beards, or faked a limp to avoid being discovered. Rudy, could you disguise yourself as a cat or a poodle?

Lots of cool tools that spies have used, like invisible ink, carrier pigeons and buttonhole cameras are on display. They even used fake dog poop to hide secret messages!

We'll learn how to sneak information across enemy lines and develop secret codes.

Real spies tell stories of eavesdropping, wire-tapping and safe-cracking: and of capture, torture and daring escapes!

We'll even see one of James Bond's cars.

photos provided by the SPY Museum

DID YOU KNOW?

A pigeon earned a medal during World War I for carrying messages to troops behind enemy lines.

Only four presidents have monuments dedicated to them...

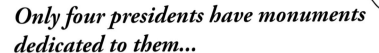

The **Washington Monument,** honoring our first president George Washington, was the first memorial built on the National Mall.

The monument is a 555-foot **"Obelisk,"** or four-sided stone pillar. It looks like a tall, really skinny pyramid.

Construction stopped in 1854 because money ran out. Twenty years later, the builders returned to work, and the triangular "capstone" was placed on the top in 1884.

DID YOU KNOW?

When builders went to finish the monument, the original quarry had run out of stone. That's why the stone at the botton of the monument is a different color.

The 50 flags at the base represent the 50 states of America.

DID YOU KNOW?

George Washington was the only president to be elected unamimously.

The Washington Monument is the **tallest** building in the city. We can take an elevator to the top and get a great view of the National Mall and the **Reflecting Pool!**

the Lincoln Memorial...

When **Abraham Lincoln** was elected president in 1860, eleven southern states tried to break away from the United States and form their own country. The North and the South fought against each other in the **CIVIL WAR** because the two sides disagreed about slavery and other issues.

President Lincoln kept the country united. He also freed millions of slaves by signing the

EMANCIPATION PROCLAMATION!

Congress passed the 13th Amendment of the US Constitution, which outlawed slavery forever.

DID YOU KNOW?

Abraham Lincoln was largely self-educated. He was also our tallest president, and he used to stash important papers under his stovepipe hat.

The Lincoln Memorial was inspired by ancient Greek temples, and it's really pretty to visit at night when it's all lit up.

Look for the words of the **GETTYSBURG ADDRESS** carved on the inside walls. Names of 48 states are carved around the outside. Alaska & Hawaii became states after the memorial was finished.

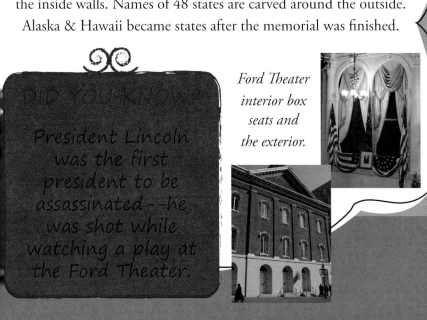

DID YOU KNOW?

President Lincoln was the first president to be assassinated--he was shot while watching a play at the Ford Theater.

Ford Theater interior box seats and the exterior.

the Jefferson Memorial...

The Jefferson Memorial is a monument to our third president, Thomas Jefferson.

Jefferson had an amazing life! He was one of the "Founding Fathers" and wrote the **DECLARATION OF INDEPENDENCE.**

He believed ALL men had the right to an education, so he created the University of Virginia. He also donated 6,487 of his own books to the **LIBRARY of CONGRESS**.

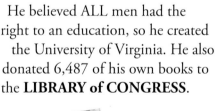

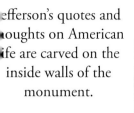

Jefferson's quotes and thoughts on American life are carved on the inside walls of the monument.

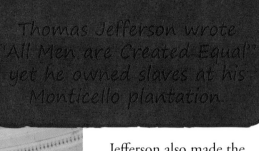

DID YOU KNOW?

Thomas Jefferson wrote "All Men are Created Equal" yet he owned slaves at his Monticello plantation.

Jefferson also made the country bigger by buying land from France in a deal called the **LOUISIANA PURCHASE**.

He sent the explorers **LEWIS & CLARK** on a big expedition to map this new western territory.

Hey Rudy, let's listen to a ranger talk here, too!

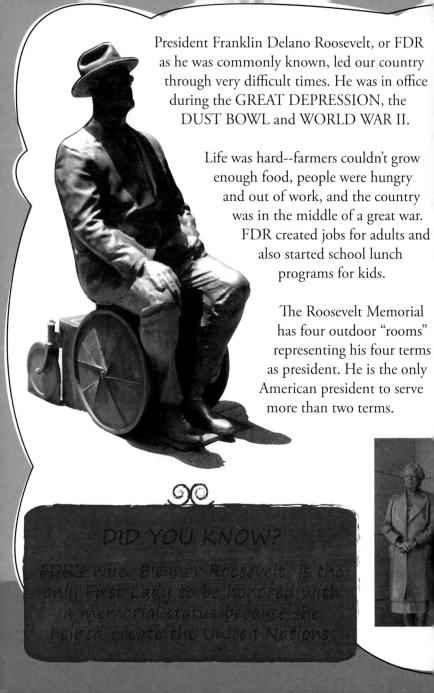

President Franklin Delano Roosevelt, or FDR as he was commonly known, led our country through very difficult times. He was in office during the GREAT DEPRESSION, the DUST BOWL and WORLD WAR II.

Life was hard--farmers couldn't grow enough food, people were hungry and out of work, and the country was in the middle of a great war. FDR created jobs for adults and also started school lunch programs for kids.

The Roosevelt Memorial has four outdoor "rooms" representing his four terms as president. He is the only American president to serve more than two terms.

DID YOU KNOW?

FDR's wife, Eleanor Roosevelt, is the only First Lady to be honored with a memorial statue because she helped create the United Nations.

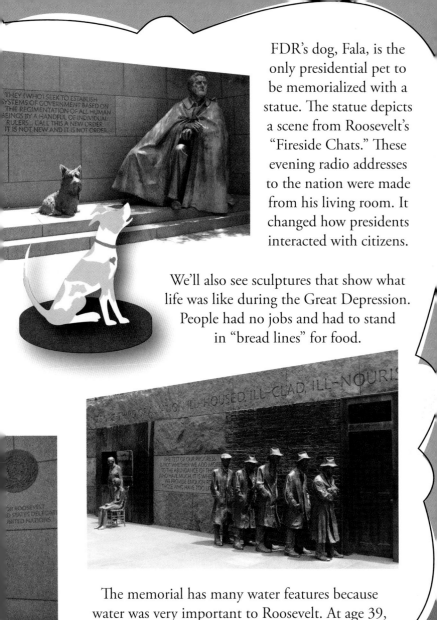

FDR's dog, Fala, is the only presidential pet to be memorialized with a statue. The statue depicts a scene from Roosevelt's "Fireside Chats." These evening radio addresses to the nation were made from his living room. It changed how presidents interacted with citizens.

We'll also see sculptures that show what life was like during the Great Depression. People had no jobs and had to stand in "bread lines" for food.

The memorial has many water features because water was very important to Roosevelt. At age 39, he got the disease called Polio and couldn't walk anymore, so he liked to swim a lot.

"*Out of a mountain of despair, a stone of hope...*"

Dr. Martin Luther King, Jr. lived at a time of terrible inequality in America. Because his skin was "colored," he wasn't allowed to eat in the same restaurants, drink from the same water fountains or use the same bathrooms as white people.

Dr. Martin Luther King, Jr. became one of the most important leaders in the CIVIL RIGHTS MOVEMENT. He organized non-violent marches that brought people of all ages and races together to protest inequality.

EQUALITY and PEACE for ALL!

*Dogs Too!

He also gave stirring talks like his **"I Have a Dream"** speech on the steps of the Lincoln Memorial in front of thousands of people.

The 30-foot statue of Dr. King is carved into the "Stone of Hope." Two big boulders on either side represent the "Mountain of Despair." These phrases are from his famous speech.

DID YOU KNOW?

The Martin Luther King Memorial is the 1st memorial on the National Mall not dedicated to a war, a president or a white man.

Around the National Mall, there are also war memorials honoring veterans from World War II, the Korean War and the Vietnam war...

World War II was the largest conflict in world history, with many countries fighting together to defeat tyranny (*teer-a-nee*).

Even kids helped by saving metal cans and old rags that were recycled and made into airplanes and uniforms.

Arlington National Cemetery holds the remains of soldiers from every US war since the Revolutionary War.

The Tomb of the Unknown Soldier and eternal flame are at Arlington Cemetery. So is the statue of Marines raising the flag at Iwo Jima during WWII.

DID YOU KNOW?

The Honor Guard takes 21 steps across the Tomb of the Unknown Soldier symbolizing the 21-gun salute.

At the Vietnam Veterans Memorial, names of the dead or missing soldiers are carved into a black granite wall to honor the men and women who served in the Vietnam War.

DID YOU KNOW?

The faces on the soldiers at the Korean War Memorial were sculpted using photographs of actual soldiers.

The Korean War Memorial honors people who served in the Korean War. 19 seven-foot steel statues depict soldiers from the Army, Marines, Air Force and Navy. The soldiers wear ponchos and stand in Juniper bushes, which symbolizes the cold winds and rice paddies of Korea.

**We've done lots of sightseeing.
Now it's time to get outside
and PLAY!**

On the **Potamac River**, we
can rent sailboats, kayaks or
paddle boards and head out
to Roosevelt Island to
explore bird life.

There are scenic boat rides
that go up the river to
MT. VERNON,
George Washington's home.

We can even ride a
PIRATE SHIP!

Did You Know?

The Japanese sent
over 3000 cherry
trees to the US in
1912 as a symbol
of friendship.

Let's play a big game
of checkers or chess
in the park at
Dupont Circle....

...or, follow signs like
the one below for an
historic walking tour.

We could go to the Tidal Basin near the
Jefferson Memorial and rent paddle boats.
In the springtime, over 3000
Japanese Cherry trees will bloom.

On hot days, we can cool down at the SPLASH PAD along the river....

...or listen to free concerts at the KENNEDY CENTE for the PERFORMING ART

Or, we cou catch a Washingto Nationals baseball gan Bring on th popcorn an hot dogs!

DID YOU KNOW?

Rock Creek Park has the only planetarium in the National Park system.

Let's go up to
ROCK CREEK PARK!
There we can hike, bike,
play tennis, go zip-lining
and horse back riding!

At Rock Creek Park's Nature Center & Planetarium,
we'll learn about astonomy at evening
STARGAZING PROGRAMS!

Rudy, now let's go to the Smithsonian National Zoo!

The animals here live together in natural groupings, just like in the wild, instead of each species being housed in a separate area.

There are more than 2000 animals here, including 400 species and over 150 different kinds of birds.

About 1/4 of the animals at the zoo are **ENDANGERED**, meaning they are in danger of disappearing from our planet completely.

Endangered species include Asian Elephants, Western Lowland Gorillas and Giant Pandas.

DID YOU KNOW?

The National Zoo was one of the first zoos to create a research program to study animals in the wild and in captivity.

We'll see Bao Bao and the other Chinese Giant Pandas that the National Zoo is known for.

Giant Pandas are hard to breed in captivity.

DID YOU KNOW?

Giant Pandas eat about 80 pounds of bamboo per day. It takes them about 12 hours to eat.

There's always something going on at the zoo!

Along the Asia Trail, we can go on a "behind-the-scenes" tour of Elephant House, or spend the night at a "SNORE & ROAR!" campout.

Don't miss the Great Ape House, the Big Cats, and the snakes and lizards at the Reptile Discovery Center!

Mount Vernon...

Mt. Vernon is George Washington's home. It's about 18 miles from downtown DC. We can bike or take a scenic boat trip up the Potomac River to get there.

Watch a movie about George and Martha's life at the Ford Orientation Center, and solve puzzles using the adventure map. Visit the Pioneer Farm where Washington grew tobacco and other crops, and tested new farming techniques.

Tour the slave cabins for a glimpse of life on the plantation.

DID YOU KNOW?

A mule is a cross between a male donkey and a female horse.

Washington is sometimes called the **"Father of the American Mule."** He liked mules better than horses for work around the farm so he started breeding them. Mules were more surefooted than horses and donkeys. They ate less food and drank less water than horses, so were cheaper to own. Washington thought they worked harder too.

If we have time, there are lots of places to visit just outside the city...

The **Yorktown Battlefield** is the site of the last major battle of the **Revolutionary War.** It's a good place to go to see what life was like for American soldiers in 1781.

Here, visit the Continental Army camp, try out a soldier's tent or join an artillery crew. We can watch military drills and learn what military field doctors did back then.

In Old Town Alexandria, we can take a tour of an old torpedo factory. It's also the place to see the

TALL SHIPS!

The **C&O Canal** starts in Georgetown and runs 184 miles to Great Falls. Take a barge ride, meet the mules, and learn about the history of this waterway that brought goods to DC for market.

The **PENTAGON** is the headquarters of the US Armed Forces and the Coast Guard. "Pentagon" means it has five sides. The Pentagon is the WORLD'S LARGEST office building--there are 18 MILES of hallways. Take a tour and visit the September 11th Memorial.

Monticello is Thomas Jefferson's country home located about two hours away in Charlottesville. In addition to being a statesman, Jefferson was also an inventor. See his copy machine and other cool inventions here.

Baltimore is just across the border in Maryland, and there are lots of fun things to do here, too.

We can take a boat out to Fort McHenry. It's a star-shaped fort that successfully defended Baltimore Harbor against the British Navy in the War of 1812.

The sight of the US flag that morning inspired Francis Scott Key to write our national anthem, the Star Spangled Banner.

Baltimore is also home to the National Acquarium! It has over 500 fish, a dolphin encounter, and the **LARGEST STINGRAY EXHIBIT** in the country.

Stingrays have barbed tails and can grow up to six and a half feet, and they look....

...just like this toy that I brought home for you.

You've been a
GOOD DOG RUDY!
while we've been gone.

Rudy's favorite things about Washington, DC are all the cool museums...

...what are <u>YOUR</u> favorite things about Washington, DC?

Match the photos above with the correct name.

A) Berlin Wall   F) Lincoln   J) Washington Monume

B) White House   G) Pentagon   K) Jefferson Monument

D) US Capitol   H) Giant Panda   L) Martin Luther King

E) Smithsonian   I) C & O Canal   M) Arlington Cemetery

TNGEA   SREDUEC

_ _ _ _ _   _ _ _ _ _ _ _

GAKECAP   NTES

_ _ _ _ _ _ _   _ _ _ _

ISSOIMN   PELTEMOC

_ _ _ _ _ _ _   _ _ _ _ _ _ _

"CODE TALKERS"

Rudy the Spy has a secret message to deliver. Can you unscramble the letters to make words and figure out the message?

Answers to all puzzles at
www.roamingwithrudy.co

WASHINGTON Puzzler

ACROSS

1. the kind of tree Japan gave to the US as a symbol of friendship
3. another name for a secret agent
6. the place where the President and his family live
7. another name for the Capitol dome
11. the huge group of museums on the National Mall
12. the study and collection of stamps

DOWN

1. the war between the north and the south
2. the dog star of this book
4. the river that flows through Washington D[
5. the first president of the United States
8. a four-sided stone pillar
9. the famous bears at the National Zoo
10. the domed building where Congress mee[

U.S. PRESIDENTS WORD SEARCH

```
M N K E N N E D Y Q H Q U W X
E D I O W F B N G T R U M A N
I R G H S B A E M R M K Q T J
S J S O T J Q D V X A S Z M E
E R P R A L A C A E R N I A F
N D A C F I I C V M J R T D F
H E P D T N I X K N S E T I E
O M T E W C N B H S V S G S R
W G D R T O I U P Q O R A O S
E T T Z F L X G T J Y N R N O
R L Z Y J N O H O B A M A T N
S U O F V G N S I I L V X R U
H Z P C A R T E R V T K R P N
R O O S E V E L T Z Q M R Q B
N W A S H I N G T O N B V J T
```

Find the following Presidents and circle them.

Washington	Jefferson	Lincoln
Roosevelt	Eisenhower	Adams
Kennedy	Jackson	Carter
Grant	Madison	Taft
Truman	Nixon	Obama

Flight Attendant Don Nay welcomes us aboard

Corinne & Rudy LOVE to travel and they hope you do too!

Corinne is the author/illustrator of three multiple award-winning children's books starring Rudy, her favorite companion and muse. Her other career as a Delta flight attendant has given her a zest for adventure, and it allows her the opportunity to roam the globe enjoying new experiences and shooting photographs for Lonely Planet Publishing and Getty Images.

With the new "Roaming with Rudy" series of KIDS-ONLY guides, Corinne and Rudy hope to share their love of travel and inspire kids to become global voyagers and cultural ambassadors.

The WORLD awaits! So get out there and explore. Here's wishing you happy journeys, many new friendships and a DOG-GONE good time!

After an abusive puppyhood, Rudy spent 3 years in and out of various shelters before I found him at Friends of Animals Utah. We donate 10% of all sales to animal rescue organizations so that other dogs can find good homes too.

bio photo by: Cheyenne Rouse

The **"Roaming with Rudy"** series
is dedicated to young travelers everywhere.
May your path be filled with
wonderful adventures,
delightful discoveries and
a DOG-GONE good time!

Thanks always
Mom & Dad for your
constant support and for introducing
me to the joys of travel!
Thank you Delta Airlines for giving
me such a fantastic opportunity
to explore the World!

Copyright 2016
Corinne Humphrey
Sage Press Books

Sage
PRESS